To
Cheryl
—*Lesléa*

To
Tootie Troy
—*Michael*

Some people are short. Some people are tall.
Some people are dark. Some people are light.
Some people are fat. Some people are thin.

Everyone looks different. My name is Daniel and this is what I look like.
My best friend's name is Belinda. This is what Belinda looks like.

Belinda and I do everything together. We play hide-and-seek and dress-up and catch.

We ride our bikes together
and go swimming...

...and sit next to each other at school.

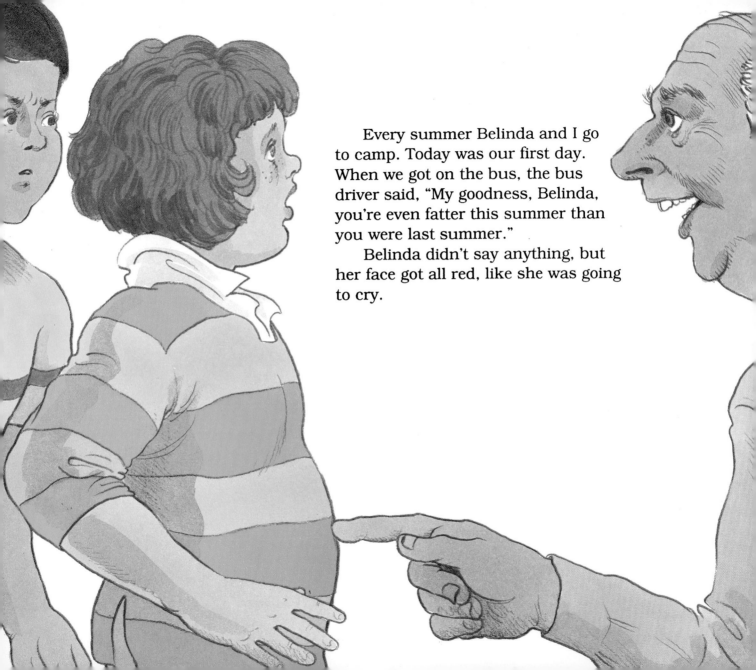

Every summer Belinda and I go to camp. Today was our first day. When we got on the bus, the bus driver said, "My goodness, Belinda, you're even fatter this summer than you were last summer."

Belinda didn't say anything, but her face got all red, like she was going to cry.

After camp, Belinda came over to my house. One of my mothers was in the kitchen, waiting for us. We told her what happened.

"Belinda, you tell that bus driver that your body belongs to you," Mama said. "It's none of anybody else's business what size your body is."

We sat down at the table and Mama poured a glass of milk for Belinda and a glass of milk for me. She gave us each three peanut butter crackers. I started eating my snack, but Belinda just sat there. "What's the matter?" I asked her. "Aren't you hungry?"

Belinda pushed her plate away. "I'm going on a diet," she said. "Maybe if I stop eating so much, I won't be fat."

Mama came over and sat down next to us. "What did you have for lunch today, Belinda?" she asked.

"I had a Swiss cheese sandwich and an apple and a glass of milk," Belinda said.

"And what did you have for lunch today?" Mama asked me.

"I had a tuna fish sandwich and a banana and a glass of milk." I looked at Belinda. "We ate the same amount," I said.

"Then how come I'm fat and you're not?" Belinda asked.

"Let me tell you a story," Mama said. "Once upon a time, there was a very wise woman who wanted to have a garden. So she put some seeds into the ground and she covered them with dirt.

"Every seed got the same amount of sunshine and every seed got the same amount of rain.

"Some of the seeds grew into short petunias, and some of the seeds grew into tall sunflowers. Some of the seeds grew into dark pansies, and some of the seeds grew into light daisies. Some of the seeds grew into fat marigolds, and some of the seeds grew into thin irises.

"Each flower was different and each flower had its own special kind of beauty. And every person has their own special kind of beauty, too."

Belinda shook her head. "I'm not beautiful," she said. "But maybe I will be after my diet."

"Let me finish my story," Mama said. "One day the very wise woman looked at her garden and she decided she wanted the short fat marigolds to be tall and thin like the irises. So she put all the marigolds on a diet.

"She only gave the marigolds half as much sunshine as all the other flowers. She only gave the marigolds half as much rain as all the other flowers."

"What happened to the marigolds?" Belinda asked. "Did they get tall and thin?"

"Oh, no," Mama said. "All their leaves started to wither and droop. They got tired and soon the poor little marigolds couldn't even hold their heads up to the sun."

"Then what happened to the marigolds?" I asked Mama.

"Then," Mama said, "the very wise woman realized she wasn't very wise at all, and it was foolish to try to make all her flowers look the same. So she gave the marigolds all the sunshine they wanted and all the water they wanted."

"Then what happened to the marigolds?" Belinda and I cried out.

"Well," Mama said, looking out the kitchen window, "I think the very wise woman is out working in her garden right now."

"Let's go see." I got up and we all ran out the door into our backyard. There was my other mother, kneeling in her flower garden, pulling up some weeds. All around her there were sunflowers and petunias and daisies and pansies and irises and hundreds and hundreds of marigolds.

"Hi, Mommy," I yelled out.

"Hi, Daniel. Hi, Belinda," Mommy yelled back.

I bent down to smell the flowers. "They're so pretty," I said. "Mommy, can we pick some?"

"Sure," Mommy said.

"Gardening is hard work," said Mama. "You need your strength. Don't you think you'd better finish your snack first?"

"C'mon," Belinda yelled, racing me back to the house. "I don't want to wither and droop."

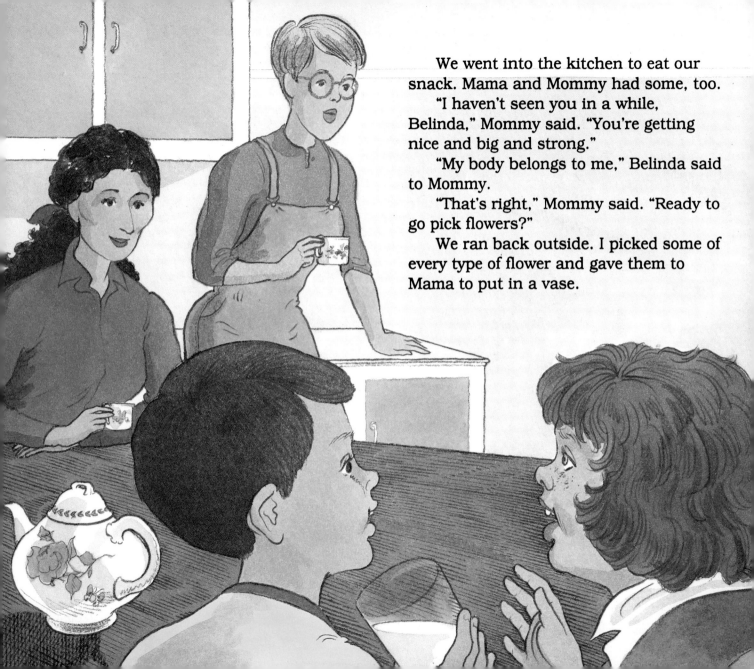

We went into the kitchen to eat our snack. Mama and Mommy had some, too.

"I haven't seen you in a while, Belinda," Mommy said. "You're getting nice and big and strong."

"My body belongs to me," Belinda said to Mommy.

"That's right," Mommy said. "Ready to go pick flowers?"

We ran back outside. I picked some of every type of flower and gave them to Mama to put in a vase.

Belinda picked as many marigolds as she could hold in her two hands and proudly carried home the fat yellow bouquet.